THE Little Red Hen

ILLUSTRATED BY Barry Downard

SIMON & SCHUSTER BOOKS FOR YOUNG READERS

New York   London   Toronto   Sydney   Singapore

SIMON & SCHUSTER BOOKS FOR YOUNG READERS
An imprint of Simon & Schuster Children's Publishing Division
1230 Avenue of the Americas, New York, New York 10020

Book design by Paula Winicur
The text for this book is set in Zapf International.
The illustrations for this book are the result of a lot of time spent taking photographs,
snaffling them up in a photo-snaffling machine, and then sticking it all together
with computer glue. No animals were hurt in the making of these images;
in fact they all had a real good time.—B. D.
Manufactured in China

2 4 6 8 10 9 7 5 3 1

Library of Congress Cataloging-in-Publication Data
The Little Red Hen / illustrated by Barry Downard.
p. cm.
Summary: When the Little Red Hen asks the other barnyard animals who
will help with the planting, reaping, and other chores, they all say,
"Not I," but when the work is done, they all want a reward.
ISBN 0-689-85962-7
[1. Folklore. 2. Animals—Folklore.] I. Downard, Barry, ill.
PZ8.1 .L72 2004
398.24'528625—dc21   2002152733

This book is dedicated to all animals everywhere.
Love them, respect them, and care for them.
After all, animals are people too.

Once upon a time there was a Little Red Hen who lived in a barnyard, along with a duck, a pig, and a cat.

One day the
Little Red Hen
found some
grains of wheat.
"Look, look!"
she clucked.
"Who will help
me plant this
wheat?"

"Not I,"
said the duck.

"Not I,"
said the pig.

"Not I,"
said the cat.

"Then I will
plant it myself,"
said the Little
Red Hen.
And she did.

The wheat grew tall and golden, and the
Little Red Hen knew that it was ready to be cut.
"Who will help me cut the wheat?" she asked.

"Not I,"
said the duck.

"Not I,"
said the pig.

"Not I,"
said the cat.

"Then I will cut it myself," said the Little Red Hen.
And she did.

"Now," said the Little Red Hen, "it is time to take this wheat to the miller, who will grind it into flour. Who will help me take the wheat to the mill?"

"Not I,"
said the duck.

"Not I,"
said the pig.

"Not I,"
said the cat.

"Then I will
take it myself,"
said the Little
Red Hen.
    And she did.

The miller ground the wheat into fine white flour and put it into a sack for the Little Red Hen. When she returned to the barnyard, the Little Red Hen asked, "Who will help me make this flour into dough?"

"Not I!" said the duck, the pig, and the cat, all at once.

"Then I will make the dough myself," said the Little Red Hen.

And she did.

When the dough was ready for baking in the oven, the Little Red Hen asked, "Who will help me bake the bread?"

"Not I,"
said the duck.

"Not I,"
said the pig.

"Not I,"
said the cat.

"Then I will
bake it all by
myself," said the
Little Red Hen.
And she did.

Bake-O-matic

Soon the white dough turned into bread. It was a delicious golden brown color and ready to be eaten. As she took it from the oven, the Little Red Hen asked, "Well, who will help me eat this warm, fresh bread?"

"I will!"
quacked the
duck.

"I will!"
oinked the pig.

"I will!"
meowed the cat.

"No, you won't," said the Little Red Hen. "You wouldn't help me plant the seeds. You wouldn't help me cut the wheat. You wouldn't help me go to the miller. You wouldn't help me make the dough. You wouldn't help me bake the bread. Now, I will eat this bread all by myself!"

And she did!